PUFFIN BOOKS

Roald Dahl's
Marvellous
Joke Book

Books by Roald Dahl

THE BFG
BOY: TALES OF CHILDHOOD
CHARLIE AND THE CHOCOLATE FACTORY
CHARLIE AND THE GREAT GLASS ELEVATOR
DANNY THE CHAMPION OF THE WORLD
GEORGE'S MARVELLOUS MEDICINE
GOING SOLO
JAMES AND THE GIANT PEACH
MATILDA
THE WITCHES

For younger readers

THE ENORMOUS CROCODILE
ESIO TROT
FANTASTIC MR FOX
THE GIRAFFE AND THE PELLY AND ME
THE MAGIC FINGER
THE TWITS

Picture books

DIRTY BEASTS *(with Quentin Blake)*
THE ENORMOUS CROCODILE *(with Quentin Blake)*
THE GIRAFFE AND THE PELLY AND ME *(with Quentin Blake)*
THE MINPINS *(with Patrick Benson)*
REVOLTING RHYMES *(with Quentin Blake)*

Teenage fiction

THE GREAT AUTOMATIC GRAMMATIZATOR AND OTHER STORIES
RHYME STEW
SKIN AND OTHER STORIES
THE VICAR OF NIBBLESWICKE
THE WONDERFUL STORY OF HENRY SUGAR AND SIX MORE

Roald Dahl's

Marvellous

Joke Book

PUFFIN

PUFFIN BOOKS

Published by the Penguin Group
Penguin Books Ltd, 80 Strand, London WC2R 0RL, England
Penguin Group (USA) Inc., 375 Hudson Street, New York, New York 10014, USA
Penguin Group (Canada), 90 Eglinton Avenue East, Suite 700, Toronto, Ontario, Canada M4P 2Y3
(a division of Pearson Penguin Canada Inc.)
Penguin Ireland, 25 St Stephen's Green, Dublin 2, Ireland (a division of Penguin Books Ltd)
Penguin Group (Australia), 250 Camberwell Road, Camberwell, Victoria 3124, Australia
(a division of Pearson Australia Group Pty Ltd)
Penguin Books India Pvt Ltd, 11 Community Centre, Panchsheel Park, New Delhi – 110 017, India
Penguin Group (NZ), 67 Apollo Drive, Rosedale, Auckland 0632, New Zealand
(a division of Pearson New Zealand Ltd)
Penguin Books (South Africa) (Pty) Ltd, Block D, Rosebank Office Park, 181 Jan Smuts Avenue,
Parktown North, Gauteng 2193, South Africa

Penguin Books Ltd, Registered Offices: 80 Strand, London WC2R 0RL, England

puffinbooks.com

First published 2012

027

Text copyright © Roald Dahl Nominee Ltd, 2012
Illustrations copyright © Quentin Blake, 2012
All rights reserved

The moral right of the author and illustrator has been asserted
Printed and bound in Great Britain by Clays Ltd, Elcograf S.p.A.

British Library Cataloguing in Publication Data
A CIP catalogue record for this book is available from the British Library

ISBN: 978–0–141–34055–5

www.greenpenguin.co.uk

Contents

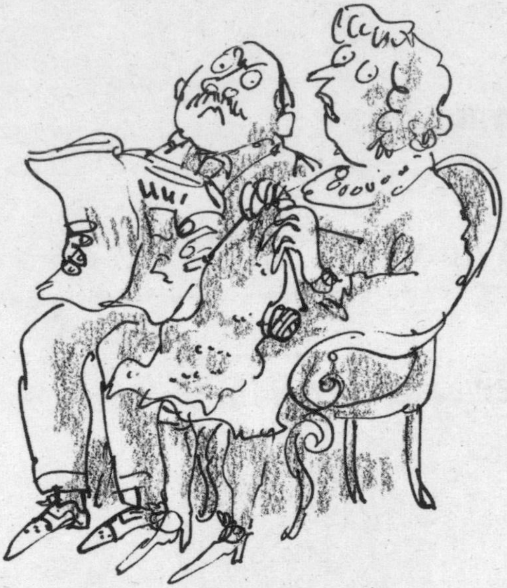

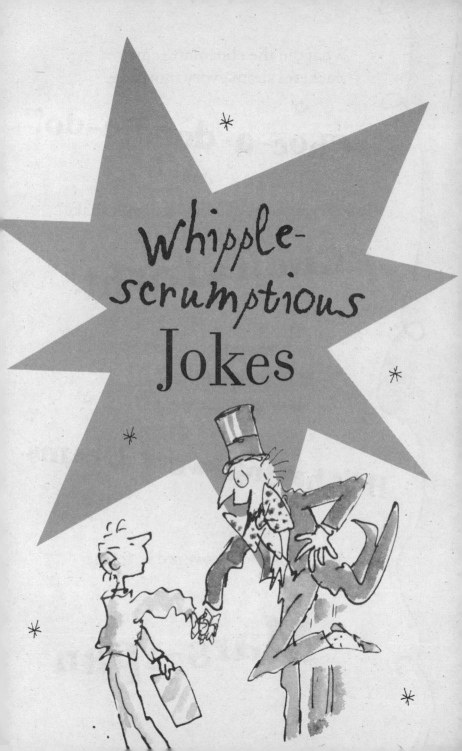

whipple-scrumptious Jokes

What did the chocolate-covered
cockerel shout every morning?

'Choc-a-doodle-do!'

How do you make a chocolate milk shake?

Give it a fright.

Why does Willy Wonka
smile when he sleeps?

He's having sweet dreams.

Which planet is covered in icing?

Mars-ipan

What's an alien's favourite snack?

A Mars bar

What do you call a well-behaved
child who steps in treacle?

Gooey Two-Shoes

Which detective solved the mystery
of the stolen sweets?

Sherbet Holmes

What do you get when you drop
a banana split from the top of a
skyscraper on to the pavement below?

A banana splat

Why did the banana
go to the doctor?

✳

Because he wasn't peeling well.

Did you hear about the storeroom
at Willy Wonka's factory that was
crammed full of chocolate bricks?

✳

It was choc-a-block.

How did the banana know it had been
in the sun too long?

✳

Its skin started to peel . . .

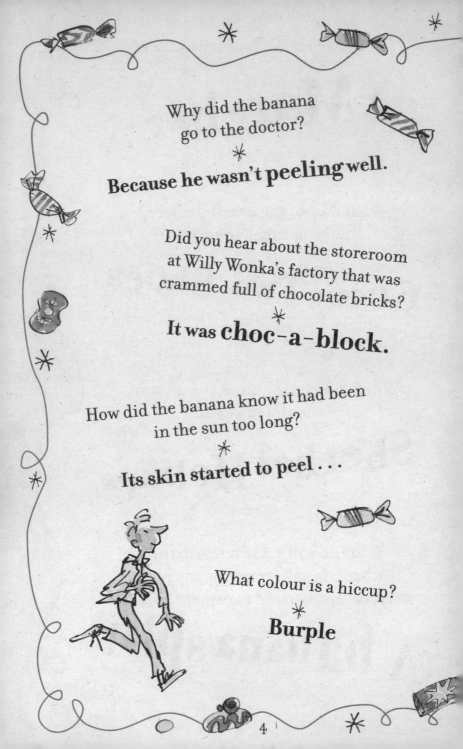

What colour is a hiccup?

✳

Burple

What does Willy Wonka use to clean his teeth?

✳

Candyfloss

What is better than a bar of Wonka's Whipple-Scrumptious Fudgemallow Delight?

✳

TWO bars of Wonka's Whipple-Scrumptious Fudgemallow Delight!

What did one strawberry say to another strawberry?

✳

'If it wasn't for you, I wouldn't be in this jam.'

What's furry and minty?

✳

A Polo bear

What is the fastest cake in the world?

Too late, it's scone.

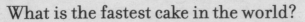

How do you turn light chocolate into dark chocolate?

Turn the light off.

Why are Brazil nuts so shy?

Because it's **hard** to get them **out** of their **shells**.

What do you call an underground train full of professors?

A tube of smarties

There was a young man
from **Bengal**,
Who was invited to a
fancy-dress ball.
He dressed up as a **bun**,
And went to the **fun**,
But a **dog** ate him **up**
in the **hall**.

What lies in a pram and wobbles?

A jelly baby!

What's bad-tempered
and goes with custard?

Apple grumble

When is a door sweet and tasty?

When it's jammed.

What's green and fluffy
and comes from Mars?

A martian mallow

What kind of sweet is always late?

A choco-late

Try saying this as fast as you can:

**A cheeky chimp chucked
cheap chocolate chips
in the cheap chocolate chip shop.**

Why don't prawns share their sweets?

Because they are shellfish.

Why are bananas good
at gymnastics?

**Because they are great
at doing the splits.**

Why did the doughnut
go to the dentist?

It needed a chocolate filling.

Two chocolate brownies are
sitting in the oven.
One turns to the other and says,
'Wow it's hot in here.'
The other brownie says,
'Whoa! A talking chocolate brownie . . .!'

Knock, knock!

Who's there?
Ice-cream soda!
Ice-cream soda who?

ICE-CREAM SODA PEOPLE

CAN HEAR ME . . .

Why did the little cookie cry?

✳

**Because his mum was
a wafer so long.**

What did the astronaut say when he
set foot on a giant chocolate bar?

✳

'I've just walked on Mars!'

What's green and hairy
and goes up and down?

✳

A gooseberry in a lift.

What do you call a chocolate-factory
owner who sits in a horse-chestnut tree?

Willy Conker!

What do Oompa-Loompas
celebrate on 31 October?

Marshmalloween!

What's made of chocolate and is
found on the sea bed?

An oyster egg

Why does your top smell of
peppermint?

Because it's a Polo shirt.

What's the best thing to put
into a chocolate pie?

Your teeth!

What did the pretty Starburst
say to the Mars bar?

'Going my Milky Way?'

What do you get if you cross a cow,
a sheep and a goat?

**The Milky
Baaa Kid!**

Why did the jelly baby go to school?

**Because he wanted to be a
Smartie.**

Why is a strawberry like a newspaper?

Because it's red all over!

What's green and hairy and shouts, 'Help! Help!'?

*

A gooseberry in a swimming pool

Why were the strawberries always late?

Because they kept getting stuck in a jam!

fantastic
Animal
Jokes

How do you know if an elephant
has been in the fridge?

You'll find its **footprints**
in the **butter**.

Which dance will a chicken NOT do?

The foxtrot

What kind of animal goes 'Oom'?

A cow walking
backwards

What do you call a pig with fleas?

Pork scratching

What do you call a donkey with
only three legs?

A Wonkey

How do farmyard animals
communicate with each other?

By walkie-turkey!

Where do sheep get their hair cut?

**At the baa-baas,
of course!**

There was a young girl called **Amba**,
Who charmed a snake called a **mamba**.
With a hypnotic glance,
She made the **snake dance**
To a **rumba**, **tango** and **samba**.

What's the difference between a
well-dressed man and a tired dog?

**One wears a suit, and
the other just pants.**

How do you catch
a squirrel?

**Climb a tree and
act like a nut.**

How do you stop a dog digging up your garden?

Take away his spade.

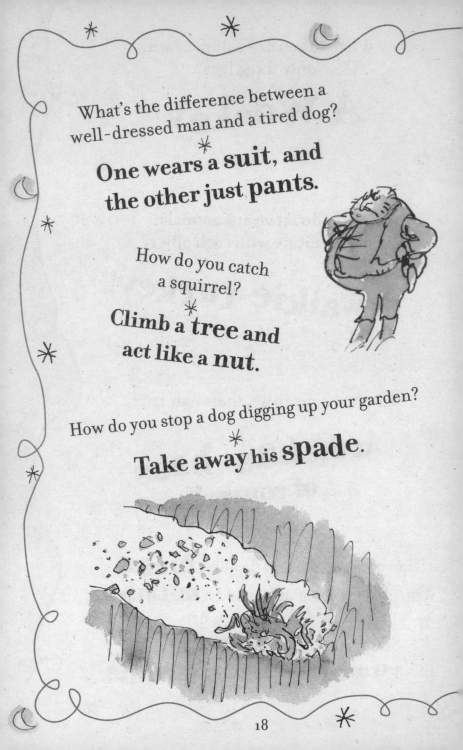

What do you call a cow that eats your grass?

A lawn-mOOer

Knock, knock!
Who's there?
Cows.
Cows who?
No, they don't. They moo.

'What happens if you
walk under a cow?'
'I don't know, what
does happen if you
walk under a cow?'

'You get a pat
on the head.'

Doctor, Doctor, I keep thinking I'm a sheep!
Really? And how do you feel about that?
Very baaaaaaadd!

Who wrote *Great Eggspectations*?

Charles Chickens

What do you get if you drop boiling water down a rabbit hole?

Hot Cross bunnies

What do you get when you put three ducks in a box?

A box of quackers

Why did the chicken
join the band?

**Because he had
the drumsticks.**

How does a chicken tell the time?

**One o'cluck, two o'cluck,
three o'cluck ...**

What's the best way
to brush your hare?

**Hold him firmly by
his long ears
and brush gently.**

What do you call a pony with a cough?

A little hoarse

What did the horse say when it fell?

'I've fallen and I can't giddyup!'

How do you save a drowning mouse?

Give it mouse-to-mouse resuscitation.

What do you get when a chicken lays an egg on top of a barn?

An eggroll

What do you get if you cross a hen with a dog?

Pooched eggs

What does a farmer talk about when he's milking cows?

Udder nonsense

How do mice celebrate when they move into a new hole?

With a mouse-warming party!

What did the parakeet say when he finished shopping?

'Just put it on my bill.'

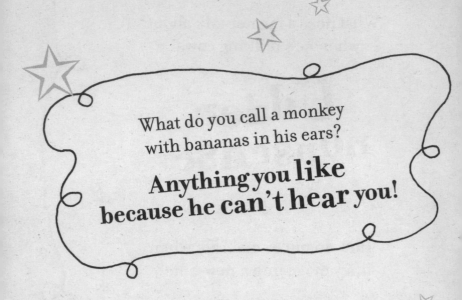

What do you call a monkey
with bananas in his ears?

**Anything you like
because he can't hear you!**

What did the farmer call his
two rows of cabbages?

A dual cabbage way

What's a rabbit's
favourite music?

Hip hop!

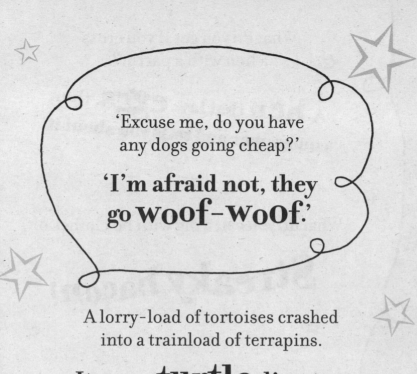

'Excuse me, do you have
any dogs going cheap?'

**'I'm afraid not, they
go woof-woof.'**

A lorry-load of tortoises crashed
into a trainload of terrapins.

It was a turtle disaster.

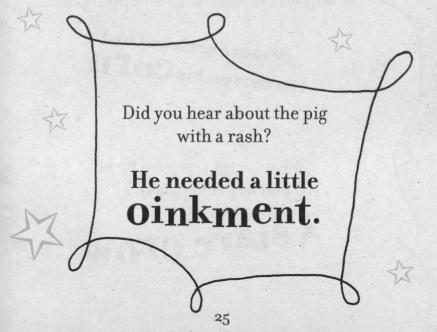

Did you hear about the pig
with a rash?

**He needed a little
oinkment.**

What do you get if you cross
a hen with a parrot?

A **hen** that lays **eggs**, then
comes over and tells you about it.

What do you call a pig with no clothes on?

Streaky bacon!

Why was Farmer Boggis hopping mad?

Because someone had
trodden on his **corn**.

What hangs around a farm
and wears big glasses?

A stare crow

What do crazy squirrels pack
their luggage in?

A nut-case

Why do birds fly south in the winter?

Because it's too far to walk!

Two sheep were in a field.
'Baaaa,' said one.
'I was going to say that!' said the other.

What happened when
the fox got arrested?

He had a brush with the law.

What's a hedgehog's favourite food?

Prickled Onions

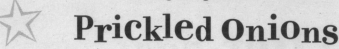

What do you get if you cross a sheepdog
with a bunch of roses?

Collie-flowers

Why did the fox cross the road?

To look for the
chicken!

Genius
Jokes

Lavender came home from school
and her dad asked if she'd had
her homework marked.

'Yes, Dad,' she replied.
'I'm afraid you didn't do very well!'

What's the fastest way to count cows?

Use a **cowculator!**

Why are adults always complaining?

Because they are
groan-ups!

Miss Honey: Can anyone tell me
where the **Andes** are?

Hortensia: I can! They're on
the end of your **armies**.

What's the difference between
Miss Trunchbull and a wild pig?

**None – they're both
a bit of a boar.**

What's a maths teacher's
favourite creature?

An adder

**Nigel came into the classroom with a great
big swelling on the end of his nose.**
'How did you get that?' asked Mr Trilby.
**'I was smelling a brose,' replied
Nigel sadly.**
'I think you mean a rose,' said Mr Trilby.
'There's no "B" in rose.'
'Well, there was in this one!'

Why are books like spies?

They are both undercover.

Which famous writer goes best with a hot dog?

Roll Dahl!

Why did Mr Trilby tell his class to shut up on the farm trip?

Because they were shouting at each udder.

What do school chips and the history class have in common?

Ancient grease

What did the nose shout out
at the school play auditions?

✳

'**Pick** me, **pick** me!'

Hortensia: I sneezed all over
Miss Trunchbull yesterday.
Matilda: How is she?
Hortensia: Snot too happy . . .

Did you hear about the nose
at the school disco?

✳

It wanted to get down and bogie!

Why did Bruce Bogtrotter eat his homework?

Because Miss Trunchbull told him it was a piece of cake.

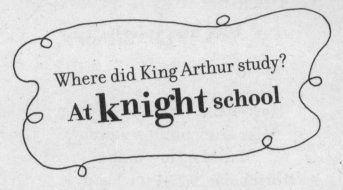

Where did King Arthur study?
At knight school

Which famous painting
never stops complaining?

The Moaner Lisa

What do elves
learn in school?

The elf-abet

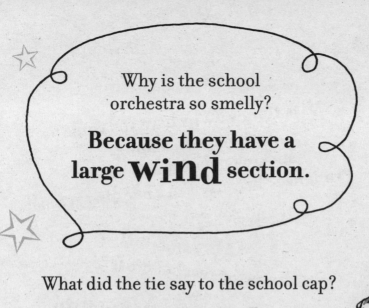

Why is the school orchestra so smelly?

Because they have a large WIND section.

What did the tie say to the school cap?

'You go on ahead while I hang around.'

Knock, knock!
Who's there?
Vanna.
Vanna who?
Vanna bunk off school?

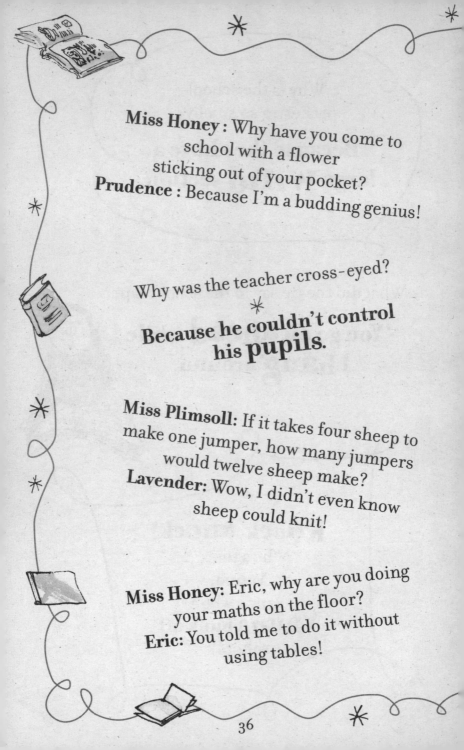

Miss Honey : Why have you come to school with a flower sticking out of your pocket?
Prudence : Because I'm a budding genius!

Why was the teacher cross-eyed?

Because he couldn't control his pupils.

Miss Plimsoll: If it takes four sheep to make one jumper, how many jumpers would twelve sheep make?
Lavender: Wow, I didn't even know sheep could knit!

Miss Honey: Eric, why are you doing your maths on the floor?
Eric: You told me to do it without using tables!

Miss Plimsoll: What do we call the outer bark of a tree?
Wilfred: Don't know, Miss.
Miss Plimsoll: Bark, silly, bark!
Wilfred: Woof, woof!

✳

Miss Honey: Make up a sentence using the word lettuce.
Nigel: Let us out of school early!

✳

Mr Trilby: The word 'politics' – can you give me an example of how to use it?
Fred: My parrot swallowed a watch and now Polly ticks!

✳

Mr Trilby: What came after the Stone Age and the Bronze Age?
Rupert: The Sausage!

A Long
Way
Down

by
Eileen Dover

Up, Up and Away!
by Ivor Kyte

Great Unanswered Questions
by Howard I Know

Grow Your Own Orchard
by Rosie Apple

Ten Years In the Saddle
by Major Burnsaw

What To Wear On Wet School Trips
by Anna Rak

Miss Trunchbull stood in front of the class and said, 'Stand up if you're an idiot.'
Hortensia stood up.
'Hortensia, why do you think you're an idiot?'
'I don't, Miss. I just hate to see you standing there all on your own!'

☆

Michael: Do you like my picture, Sir? It's a bunch of cows.
Mr Trilby: Herd of cows.
Michael: Of course I've heard of cows – do you think I'm stupid or something?

☆

Why did Wilfred study in an aeroplane?

He wanted a higher education!

☆

What do you call a clever girl who's an expert ballroom dancer?

Waltzing Matilda!

What do pigs play in the school playground?

Leap-hog!

What did Miss Trunchbull say to the boy with a gherkin in each nostril?

'Stop pickling your nose!'

Where does a school keep all the books that aren't true?

In the lie-brary

What do you do if a teacher rolls her eyes at you?

Pick them up and roll them back to her!

Why is the maths book so unhappy?

Because it's full of problems.

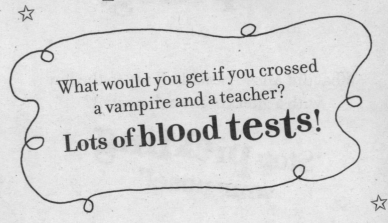

What would you get if you crossed
a vampire and a teacher?

Lots of blood tests!

Have you heard about the class joker who put
washing powder in the head teacher's coffee?
Was he angry?
Angry? He was **foaming** at the mouth!

Disgusting
Silly Twit
Jokes

Why did the toilet paper roll
down the hill?

To get to the **bottom**.

Did you hear about the cruel chef?

He **beats** the eggs
and **whips** the cream!

What happens when
the Queen burps?

She issues a
royal pardon.

What's yellow and smells
of bananas?

Monkey sick

What's worse than finding a
caterpillar in your apple?

Finding **half** a **caterpillar**
in your apple . . .

What's the difference between
Mr Twit and a cowpat?

A **cowpat** stops being
smelly after a couple of days.

What did one smelly sock
say to the other smelly sock?

*

**'Are you stinking
what I'm stinking?'**

What happened to the boy who
drank eight cans of Coke?

*

He brought 7 up.

What did one toilet
say to another toilet?

*

**You look a bit
flushed.**

Knock, knock!
Who's there?
Twit.
Twit who?
I don't speak owl, let me in!

What's grey and hairy and
lives on a man's face?

A mousetache

How many rotten eggs does it
take to make a stink bomb?

A phew!

There was an old man with a **beard**,
Who said, 'It is just as I **feared!**
Two owls and a **hen**,
Four larks and a **wren**,
Have all built their **nests** in my **beard**!'
(by Edward Lear)

What do you get if you cross
a worm and a young goat?

A dirty kid

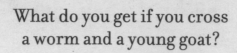

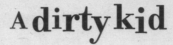

What's green and slimy and found
at the North Pole?

A lost frog!

What did the slug say as he
slipped down the wall?

'How **slime flies.**'

What do you call a girl
with a frog in her hair?

Lily!

Why do giraffes have long necks?

Because they've got smelly feet.

How do you stop a skunk from smelling?

Hold on to its nose.

What's the difference between broccoli and bogies?

Kids will eat bogies...

What do you call a fairy
who hasn't taken a bath?

Stinkerbell

What is a skeleton?

Bones with the person off

What do you get when you cross
a skunk with a teddy bear?

Winnie the Phew!

Where did the spaghetti go to dance?

The meat ball

What do you do to find your lost pet monkey?

Hide in a tree and make a **noise** like a **banana!**

What did the banana say to the monkey?

Nothing. Bananas don't talk.

What do chimpanzees like to eat?

Choc-chimp cookies

What's brown and sticky?
*
A stick!

What's yellow,
brown and hairy?
*
**Cheese on toast
stuck on the carpet**

What do you do if you find a
python in your toilet?
*
Wait until he's finished . . .

What's black and white and green?
*
A zebra with a runny nose

What's the only kind of poo
that doesn't smell horrible?

✳

Shampoo

What comes from the desert and shouts 'Bum!'?

✳

Crude oil

What has a bottom at its top?

✳

A leg!

A man goes to the doctor and he
has a banana sticking out of each
ear and a sweetcorn up his nose.
'Doctor, I don't feel very well.'
'Well, you're clearly not eating right!'

How do chimps make toast?

✳

They use a gorilla.

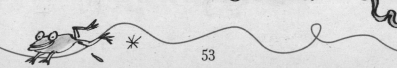

Doctor, Doctor, I've got a
carrot growing in my ear!

How did that happen?

I don't know — I planted
cauliflowers!

☆

What's brown and sits on a piano stool?

Beethoven's
last movement

☆

Doctor, Doctor, I've got too much
fluff in my belly button.

That's good. I've been wanting to
re-stuff my couch for ages!

☆

Why did the boy take
toilet paper to the party?

**Because he was a
party pooper!**

What do you get when you cross a rooster, a dog and something gross?

A cockle-poodle-eeew!

What has a sweet taste and flies?

A lollipop left out in the garden

Why did the monkey lie on the sunbed?

To get an orangutan!

What did one toilet roll say to the other toilet roll?

'I can't tear myself away from you.'

What's invisible and smells like bananas?

Monkey burps

What did one eye say to the other?

'Between you and me, something smells.'

What monkey looks like a flower?

A chimp-pansy

Creepy-
crawly
Jokes

What do you get if you cross a
centipede and a parrot?

A walkie-talkie!

What does a caterpillar
do on New Year's Day?

Turns over a
new leaf!

What goes ninety-nine-clonk, ninety-
nine-clonk, ninety-nine-clonk?

A centipede with
a wooden leg!

What do you get if you
cross a rabbit and a flea?

Bugs Bunny!

What did Mr Flea say
to Mrs Flea?
'I love you **aw-flea!**'

What is the difference between
a flea and a wolf?

One **prowls** on the hairy and the
other **howls** on the prairie.

Why is it better to be a
grasshopper than a cricket?

Because **grasshoppers** can
play cricket, but **crickets**
can't play grasshopper.

Why was the glow-worm unhappy?

Because her children
weren't that **bright**...

Knock, knock!
Who's there?
Amos.
Amos who?
Amos-quito bit me!

Why was the caterpillar
embarrassed?
✳
Because the centi-peed.

What did one centipede say
to the other centipede?
✳

'You've got a lovely pair of **legs**,
a **lovely** pair of legs,
a lovely **pair** of legs,
a lovely pair of **legs**,
a **lovely** pair of legs,
a lovely **pair** of legs . . .!'

Waiter, what is this fly doing in my soup?

I think it's doing breaststroke, sir!

Waiter, there's a grasshopper in my soup!

Yes, sir, it's the fly's day off.

Two flies were playing football in a saucer.

They were practising for the cup!

What did one flea say to the other when they were on the dog's back?

'I'll hang around here fur a while, you go on a head!'

What do insects learn at school?

Mothematics

Why couldn't the two worms
in an apple get on Noah's Ark?

**Because everyone had
to go on in pairs . . .**

What is a grasshopper?

**An insect on a
pogo stick**

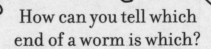

How can you tell which
end of a worm is which?

**Tickle it in the
middle and see
which end laughs!**

Why was the centipede
dropped from the football team?

**He took too long to
put his boots on.**

What do you get if you cross
a tarantula with a rose?

**I'm not sure,
but I wouldn't try
smelling it!**

What is the definition
of a caterpillar?

**A worm in a
fur coat!**

What is a glow-worm's favourite food?

Anything, so long as it's just a
light snack.

What's black, yellow and
covered in blackberries?

A bramble bee

What do you call a swarm
of monster bees?

Zombees

What kind of suit does a bee
wear for work?

A buzzness
suit

Why was the knight afraid of the bug?

Because it was a dragonfly.

What did the bee say to the other bee?

'It's none of your buzzness.'

What do you call a cheerful flea?

A hop-timist!

What did the clean dog say to the insect?

'Long time no flea!'

What is red and dangerous?

**Strawberry and
tarantula jelly!**

What do you get if you cross a
spider and an elephant?

**I'm not sure, but if you see one
walking across the ceiling
then run before it falls down!**

Why did the bees go on strike?

**Because they wanted
more honey and shorter
working flowers!**

What did the spider say to the fly?

'We're getting married – do you want to come to the webbing?'

There was a young lady called Palmer
Who became quite an expert
snake **charmer**.
The snakes called her Miss
And gave a loud **hiss**
When it looked as if someone
would harm her.

What is the difference
between a fly and a bird?

A bird can fly, but a fly can't bird . . .

What did the spider say to the bee?

Your honey or your life!

'I must fly,' said the bluebottle.
'OK,' said the bee. 'I'll give
you a **buzz** later.'

What is a slug's favourite drink?

Slime Cordial

What is the most faithful insect?

A flea – once they find
someone they like to
stick to them.

What is green and can jump
a mile in a minute?

A grasshopper
with hiccups

When do snails go inside
their homes?

**When they need
shell-ter...**

What kind of fly spends all
its time complaining?

A bitter fly!

Why couldn't the butterfly
go to the dance?

**Because it was a
moth-ball.**

Did you hear about the two
silkworms who had a race?

It ended in a tie.

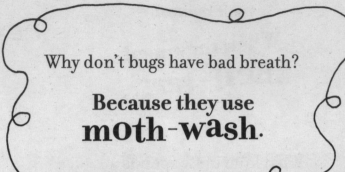

Why don't bugs have bad breath?

**Because they use
moth-wash.**

Two fleas were running across
the top of a cereal packet.
'Why are we running so fast?' said one.
'Because it says,

**"Tear along
the dotted line."'**

Phizz-whizzing Witch Jokes

An old witch thought she would
make a fortune telling fortunes,
so she bought a crystal ball, but
she couldn't see any future in it!

What do you get if you cross
an owl with a witch?

**A bird that's ugly but
doesn't give a hOot!**

What do witches eat at Halloween?

**Spooketti
and boo-berry pie**

What witch is good when it's dark?

A light switch

What happened to the witch
with an upside-down nose?

Every time she sneezed
her hat blew off.

I met two witches who were twins.

But I just couldn't tell which
witch was which!

What is evil and ugly on the
inside, and green on the outside?

A witch dressed
as a cucumber!

What is evil, ugly and goes
round and round?

A witch in a revolving door!

What is black, old and ugly and has four wheels?

A witch on a skateboard!

Why wasn't there any food left after the witch's party?

Because everyone was a goblin.

What do witches use to stop getting sunburnt?

Suntan potion!

What kinds of tests do they give witches?

Hex-aminations and spelling tests!

Why do witches fly around
on broomsticks?
*
**Because vacuum cleaners
are too heavy.**

Who did the
wizard marry?
*
His ghoul-friend!

What sound does a witch's cereal make?
*
Snap, cackle and pop!

What does a witch get if she is a poor traveller?

Broom-sick!

Have you heard about the good weather witch?

She's forecasting sunny spells.

What do you call a nervous witch?

A twitch

What do you get when you cross a witch with an ice cube?

A cold spell

What does a witch ask for in a hotel?

Broom service

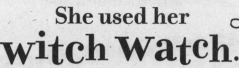
How did the witch know it
was exactly twelve midday?
**She used her
witch Watch.**

Why are witches good at English?
**Because they are
brilliant at spelling.**

What do you give a witch at tea-time?
A cup and sorcerer

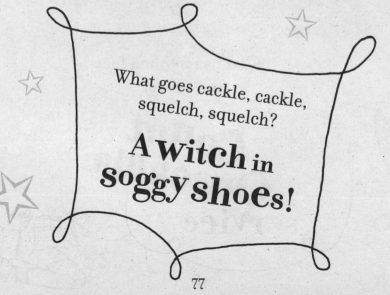
What goes cackle, cackle,
squelch, squelch?
**A witch in
soggy shoes!**

What do you call a
witch's motorbike?

A baaarrroooOoomstick!

Knock, knock!
Who's there?
Gruesome.
Gruesome who?
I like flowers so I gruesome.

What has webbed feet
and fangs?

Count
Quackula

What witches do you
find in the desert?

Sandwitches

What do witches like to read at bedtime?

Ghoul Deluxe
and the
Three Scares

What feature do witches love
having on their computers?

A spell-
checker

What did the doctor
say to the witch?

✳

'With any luck you'll
soon be well enough to
get up for a spell!'

What are crisp, like milk and go
'eek, eek, eek' when you eat them?

✳

Mice Krispies!

What is small, furry and
brilliant at sword fights?

✳

A mouseketeer!

How did the witch know
that she was ill?

She had a dizzy spell.

What's the biggest mouse in the world?

A **hippo**potamouse!

What do witches wear to bed?

Fright-gowns

What do witches use to keep
their hair looking nice?

Scare spray!

How does a witch relax?

In a hubble bubble bath

Why did the angry witch
land with a bump?

Because she lost her temper and flew off the handle.

What does an Australian
witch ride on?

A boomerang

Is it good to drink witch's brew?

Yes, it's very newt-ricous!

What happened to the naughty little witch at school?

She got ex-spelled!

Why did the witch keep turning people into Mickey Mouse?

Because she was having Disney spells.

What do you call a witch who likes the beach but is scared of the water?

A chicken sandwitch

What's the most important rule for witches?

Don't fly off the handle.

Why couldn't the witch sing
Christmas carols?

**Because of the
frog in her throat.**

Why do witches wear pointy hats?

**To keep their
pointy heads warm.**

Marvellous Family Jokes

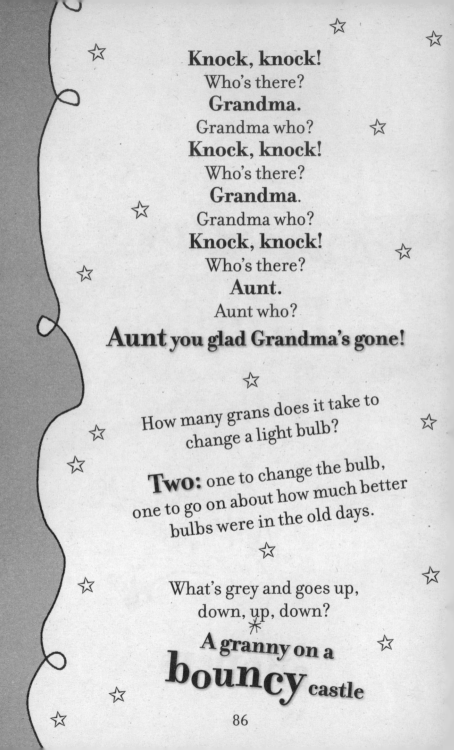

Knock, knock!
Who's there?
Grandma.
Grandma who?
Knock, knock!
Who's there?
Grandma.
Grandma who?
Knock, knock!
Who's there?
Aunt.
Aunt who?

Aunt you glad Grandma's gone!

☆

How many grans does it take to
change a light bulb?

Two: one to change the bulb,
one to go on about how much better
bulbs were in the old days.

☆

What's grey and goes up,
down, up, down?

A granny on a
bouncy castle

What does 'minimum' mean?

A very small mother!

What does 'maximum' mean?

A very big mother!

Mum, why is Grandma wearing two banana skins on her feet?

She wanted a new pair of slippers.

Did you hear about the father who drowned in a bowl of muesli?

A strong currant pulled him under.

Mum, I feel as sick as a dog.

Oh dear, I'd better call the vet.

Distraught granny: Our cat's gone missing!
Policeman: Why don't you put an ad in the newspaper?
Distraught granny: Don't be silly — Sooty can't read!

Did you hear about the stupid boy who tried to make his sister a birthday cake?

The candles melted in the oven.

Mummy, I had a terrible dream a man in a tin suit was chasing me!

There, there, dear — it was only a knightmare.

What music do dads
and alligators listen to?

Croc 'n' Roll

George: Dad, what are those holes
in the wood?
Mr Kranky: They're knotholes.
George: Well, if they're not holes,
what are they?

Why was the Egyptian girl worried?

Because her daddy was a mummy!

Who carries a basket,
visits Grandma and
steals her jewellery?

Little Red Robin Hood

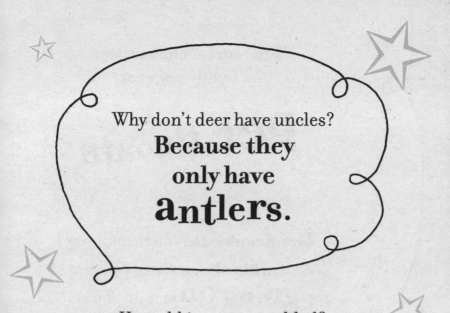

Why don't deer have uncles?
Because they only have antlers.

How old is your granddad?
I don't know, but we've had him a long time!

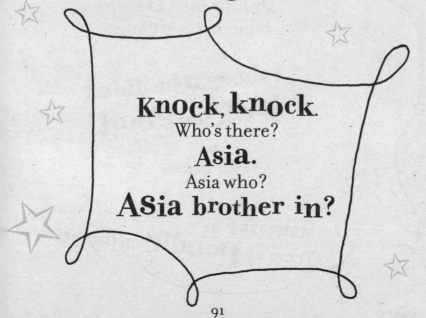

Knock, knock.
Who's there?
Asia.
Asia who?
Asia brother in?

What sort of clothes does
the family pet wear?

Pet-ticoats

Mrs Kranky: Do you think I nag?

Mr Kranky: No, but can you please
stop **going on** and on about it…?

My little brother keeps
bumping into things.

**I thought he didn't
look too good.**

Mum, the dog's been naughty again.
There's a **poodle** on the carpet!

Why don't you take your
little brother to the zoo?

**If they want him,
they can come
and get him!**

My granny has teeth like stars.
Really?
Yes, they **come out** at night.

Mrs Kranky: Doctor, I'm extremely
worried about my husband. He keeps
thinking he's turned into a **chicken**.
Doctor: Why didn't you tell me
this before?
Mrs Kranky: Well, we've needed
the **eggs** . . .

Do you know why my little brother
is built upside down?

✳

**Because his nose runs
and his feet smell.**

Mrs Kranky: Why have you got a
sausage behind your ear?

✳

Mr Kranky: Oh dear, I must have
eaten my pencil for breakfast.

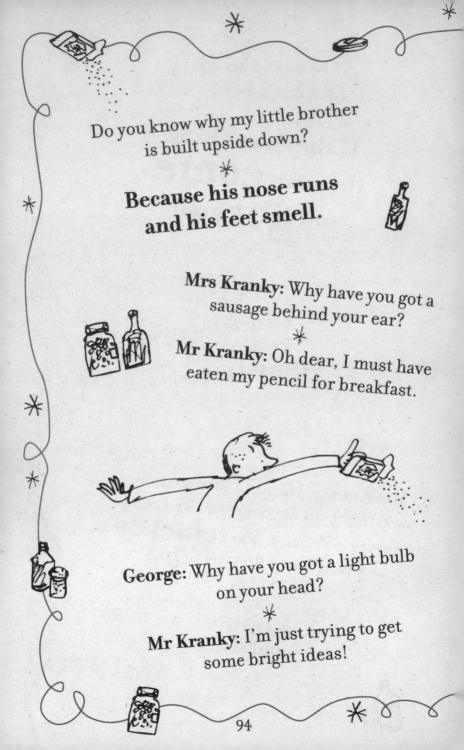

George: Why have you got a light bulb
on your head?

✳

Mr Kranky: I'm just trying to get
some bright ideas!

My brother is so silly he thinks that **barnacles** are where **seahorses** live.

Mrs Kranky: Why does your dad jump up and down before taking his medicine?

*

George: Because he read the label, and it said, 'Shake well before using.'

Dad, I ate the dictionary!

*

Don't breathe a word to your mother!

Did you hear about the magician who sawed people in half?

*

He had lots of half-brothers and sisters.

**Doctor, Doctor! My aunty
thinks she's an elevator.**

Tell her to come in.

I can't. She doesn't stop at this floor.

George: Dad, can you help me with
my science homework?

Mr Kranky: I could, but it wouldn't be right.

George: I don't suppose so, but you could
try anyway . . .

When should you put a
spider in your sister's bed?

**When you can't
find a frog…**

Grandma wanted to visit her
daughter who lived in Australia.
She rang the airline and
asked how long it would take.
'Just a minute,' came the reply.
'Really? I thought it would take
longer than that!' said Grandma.

What song did they play when
the baker got married?

Here **Crumbs** the bride!

☆

How does Batman's mother
call him for dinner?

'Dinner, dinner, dinner,
dinner, dinner,
dinner, dinner,
dinner, **Batman!**'

☆

Who was bigger, Mr Bigger or his son?

His son . . . he was a little
Bigger.

☆

What do you get when you cross
a grandma and an octopus?

I don't know but it can
sure play **bingo!**

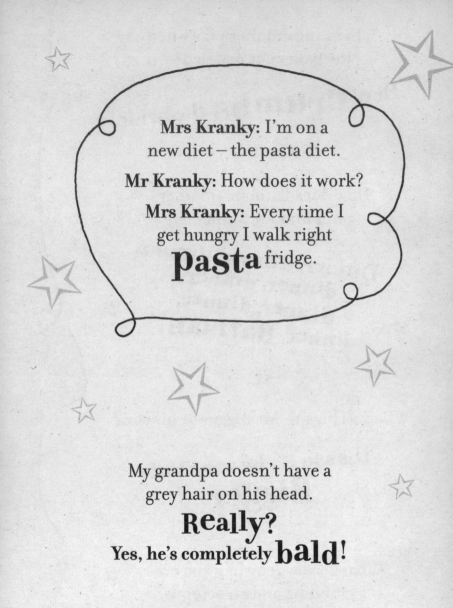

Mrs Kranky: I'm on a new diet – the pasta diet.

Mr Kranky: How does it work?

Mrs Kranky: Every time I get hungry I walk right **pasta** fridge.

My grandpa doesn't have a grey hair on his head.

Really?

Yes, he's completely **bald**!

Whoppsy-whiffling Giant Jokes

Knock, knock

Who's there?

Boo.

Boo who?

There, there, giants don't cry.

The giant could smell a human a mile away and he knew that there was an intruder in the castle. The gates were locked, so how had the human got inside?

Intruder window!

What should you do after shaking hands with a giant?

Count your fingers.

What do giants have for lunch at school?

Human beans, boiled **legs**, pickled **bunions** and **eyes**-cream.

On which day do giants eat people?

Chewsday

Why did the Jolly Green Giant get kicked out of the garden?

Because he took a pea!

What is a giant's favourite game?

Swallow the leader!

What do you call a giant
in a phone box?

Stuck

What do you call a giant with
carrots in his ears?

**Anything you want –
he can't hear you.**

Why did the giant ape climb up the
side of the skyscraper?

The lift was broken!

What do you call a giant with a
tree growing out of his head?

Ed-wood

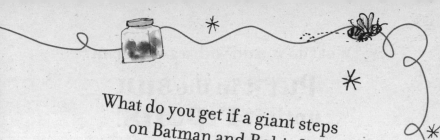

What do you get if a giant steps
on Batman and Robin?

*

Flatman and Ribbon!

What goes 'ha-ha-bonk'?

*

A giant laughing his head off.

What's green and
goes up and down?

*

A snozzcumber in a lift!

Did you hear about the giant with
one eye at the back of his head,
and one at the front?

*

He was upset because he couldn't see eye to eye with himself.

What do you do with a green giant?

**Put it in the sun
until it ripens!**

What happens if a big, hairy giant
sits in front of you at the cinema?

**You miss most
of the film.**

What did the big, hairy giant
do when he lost a hand?

**He went to the
secondhand shop.**

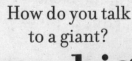

How do you talk
to a giant?

**Use big
words.**

Did you hear about the
giant burglar who fell in
the cement mixer?

**Now he's a
hardened
criminal.**

What did the giant order
in the restaurant?

The waiter!

Why don't giants eat clowns?

**Because they
taste funny.**

Why did the one-eyed giant
close his school?

Because he only had
one pupil.

What do you call a flea that
lives in a giant's ear?

A space invader!

Where do you find giant snails?

At the end of giants' fingers!

What do you call a giant
with a bucket and spade?

Doug

What's green and wears a mask?

The Lone Snozzcumber

Why did the snozzcumber need a lawyer?

Because it was in a pickle.

What's a giant's favourite
ball game?

Squash

Where should a 500-tonne giant go?

On a diet!

Mother Giant: How many times
have I told you not to eat
with your fingers?

**Use the spade like
everyone else.**

What do you get if you cross a plum
with a man-eating giant?

A purple people-eater

What does a mother giant say
to her children at lunchtime?

✳

**Don't talk with someone
in your mouth.**

What is a giant's
favourite tale?

✳

A tall story!

What steps would you take if
a giant approached you?

✳

Great big ones!

What do you call a giant with two
noses, three eyes and only one ear?

✳

Very ugly!

What's a giant's favourite meal?

Kate and Sidney pie

Knock, knock!
Who's there?
Sarah.
Sarah who?
Sarah a giant living here?

What do you do if a giant
runs off with your football?

Buy another one...

What does a polite giant say when
he meets you for the first time?

**'Pleased to
eat you!'**

How do you tell a good
giant from a bad one?

If it's a **good** one, you'll be
able to talk about it later.

What do you get if you cross a
green giant with a fountain pen?

The **Ink-credible
Hulk!**

How do you stop a giant from smelling?

Cut off his nose.

What did the giant say when he saw a
rush-hour train full of passengers?

'Oh goody, a **chew-
chew train!**'

And finally...

What time is it when a
giant sits on a fence?

Time to get a
new fence.

SURPRISE

Bet you thought this book had finished.
Well, here's some truly marvellous news – it hasn't!
Turn the page for a whole load of Roald Dahl treats.

YIPPPPEEEE!

GOBBLEFUNK

Roald Dahl loved playing around with words and inventing new ones. In *The BFG* he gave this strange language an even stranger name – Gobblefunk!

BLABBERSNITCH

A creature that lives at the bottom of the sea.

CRODSCOLLOP

A mouth-watering flavour; for example, the taste of chocolate ice cream.

BUGGLES

Means completely crazy!

GOGGLER

An eye.

OOMPA-LOOMPA

A very small person. A tribe of them work in Willy Wonka's fantastic chocolate factory.

HORNSWOGGLER

A very dangerous creature.

PHIZZ-WHIZZING

Means brilliant or really, really good!

RINGBELLER

The BFG's word for an amazingly excellent dream; the complete opposite of a nightmare.

SPLATCH-WINKLE

Splatch-winkling means rushing around; in a hurry.

SVOLLOP

To svollop something means to destroy it.

TIME-TWIDDLER

A time twiddler is very special. Time-twiddlers are immortal; they live forever and ever.

VERMICIOUS KNID

Watch out! These beasts are vicious killers who can fool you by changing shape.

WHOOPSY-SPLUNKERS

Used to describe something absolutely marvellous.

Roald Dahl's
PUFFIN PASSPORT

Autograph	*Roald Dahl*
Birthday	13 September, 1916
Colour of eyes	Blue-grey
Colour of hair	Greyish
Special virtue	Never satisfied with what I've done.
Special vice	Drinking
Favourite colour	Yellow
Favourite food	Caviar

Favourite music   Beethoven

Favourite personality   My wife and children

Favourite sound   Piano

Favourite TV programme   News

Favourite smell   Bacon frying

Favourite book when young   "Mr. Midshipman Easy"

If I wasn't an author I'd like to be   A Doctor

My most frightening moment   In a Hurricane, 1941,
                                                    R.A.F.

My funniest moment   Being born

Motto

My candle burns at both ends
It will not last the night
But ah my foes and oh my friends
It gives a lovely light.

Roald Dahl's
FAVOURITE THINGS

There was a table in the writing hut on which Roald Dahl kept
his collection of special things. And they're all still there.

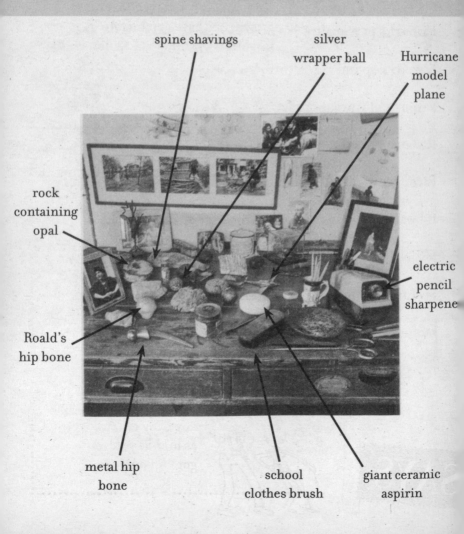

spine shavings

silver
wrapper ball

Hurricane
model
plane

rock
containing
opal

electric
pencil
sharpene

Roald's
hip bone

metal hip
bone

school
clothes brush

giant ceramic
aspirin

ROALD DAHL SAYS

'I think probably kindness is my number one attribute in a human being. I'll put it before any of the things like courage or bravery or generosity or anything else. If you're kind, that's it.'

'I am totally convinced that most grown-ups have completely forgotten what it is like to be a child between the ages of five and ten . . . I can remember exactly what it was like. I am certain I can.'

'When I first thought about writing the book *Charlie and the Chocolate Factory*, I never originally meant to have children in it at all!'

'If I had my way, I would remove January from the calendar altogether and have an extra July instead.'

'You can write about anything for children as long as you've got humour.'

THERE'S MORE TO ROALD DAHL THAN GREAT STORIES . . .

Did you know that 10% of Roald Dahl's royalties* from this book go to help the work of the Roald Dahl charities?

Roald Dahl's Marvellous Children's Charity aims to raise as much money as possible to make seriously ill children's lives better because it believes that every child has the right to a marvellous life. This marvellous charity helps thousands of children each year in the UK living with serious conditions of the blood and the brain — causes important to Roald Dahl in his lifetime.

Whether by providing nurses, equipment, carers or toys, the charity helps to care for children with conditions including acquired brain injury, epilepsy and blood disorders such as sickle cell disease. Can you do something marvellous to help others?

Find out how at **www.marvellouschildrenscharity.org**

The Roald Dahl Museum and Story Centre, based in Great Missenden just outside London, is in the Buckinghamshire village where Roald Dahl lived and wrote. At the heart of the Museum, created to inspire a love of reading and writing, is his unique archive of letters and manuscripts. As well as two fun-packed biographical galleries, the Museum boasts an interactive Story Centre. It is a place for the family, teachers and their pupils to explore the exciting world of creativity and literacy.

Find out more at **www.roalddahlmuseum.org**

It all started with a Scarecrow.

Puffin is seventy years old.
Sounds ancient, doesn't it? But Puffin has never been
so lively. We're always on the lookout for the next big
idea, which is how it began all those years ago.

Penguin Books was a big idea from the mind of
a man called Allen Lane, who in 1935 invented
the quality paperback and changed the world.
**And from great Penguins, great Puffins grew,
changing the face of children's books forever.**

The first four Puffin Picture Books were hatched in 1940 and the
first Puffin story book featured a man with broomstick arms called
Worzel Gummidge. In 1967 Kaye Webb, Puffin Editor, started the
Puffin Club, promising to 'make children into readers'.
She kept that promise and over 200,000 children became
devoted Puffineers through their quarterly instalments of
Puffin Post, which is now back for a new generation.

Many years from now, we hope you'll look back and
remember Puffin with a smile. **No matter what your age
or what you're into, there's a Puffin for everyone.**
The possibilities are endless, but one thing is for sure:
whether it's a picture book or a paperback, a sticker book
or a hardback, **if it's got that little Puffin
on it – it's bound to be good.**